It Chanced to Rain
Kathleen Bullock

Simon and Schuster Books for Young Readers
Published by Simon & Schuster Inc., New York

For Patrick, Amy, and Mary

Library of Congress Cataloging-in-Publication Data
Bullock, Kathleen. 1946— It chanced to rain / written and illustrated by Kathleen Bullock. p.   cm. Summary: Three rats, three ducks, three dogs,
and three cats go out for a walk with two young pigs; but, when it starts to rain, they rush back home only to find that the ducks are missing.
[1. Animals — Fiction.   2. Stories in rhyme.]   I. Title. PZ8.3.B89 It   1989   [E] — dc19   87-32070 CIP AC
ISBN 0-671-66005-5

Three young Rats in black felt hats,

Three young Ducks in white straw flats,

Three young Dogs with upturned tails,

Three young Cats in hats with veils

Went out to walk with two young Pigs
In satin vests and curly wigs,

When suddenly it chanced to rain

And so they all went home again.

The way back home was very long.
The rain fell hard; the wind blew strong.
But down the path they hurried, splashing.
Thunder clouds above were flashing!

They ran a country mile or more,
Then came at last to their front door.

(They must have been *drenched*!)

The first young Pig wiped every nose.
The second took their soggy clothes,
And threw them dripping in the dryer.
The rest stood huddled by the fire.

And, for the fourteen, each a chair,
But wait! The Ducklings were not there!

And, though they hunted all around,

The three young Ducks could not be found.
(Where *could* they be?)

In plastic coats and rubber hats,
The Pigs went out with the Dogs and Cats.
The little Rats were left alone
To listen for the telephone.

Perhaps the Ducks were hurt or lost!
They must be found at any cost.

They searched the country high and low
In every place a Duck might go,
Then saw a sight that made them shiver:
Three hats were drifting down the river!

"Oh dear, they've drowned!" cried out the Cats,
"And left us nothing but their hats!"
They cried because their feathered friends
Had met with such unhappy ends.

Then 'round the rushes, into sight,
Swam three young Ducklings, faces bright.
"A rainstorm's *our* idea of fun!
We've had a fling and now we're done."

(Well! Very thoughtless of the Ducks
to give their friends such a scare!)

Later...Three sniffly Cats with fur all wet

And three sneezy Dogs went to the vet.

The three young Rats, with noses red,
Caught the snuffles and went to bed.

The two young Pigs, tired but wise,
Put up their feet and closed their eyes.

But the three young Ducks at the end of the day
Had to wash the dishes and put them away.

(And wasn't that just *too* bad!)